To my precious family—thank you for teaching
me the importance of being faithful with
"little" and with "much."

– Erika

To Micah, Hannah, and James.

– Josh

THE SAVING FARMER
Published by David C Cook
4050 Lee Vance Drive
Colorado Springs, CO 80918 U.S.A.

David C Cook U.K., Kingsway Communications
Eastbourne, East Sussex BN23 6NT, England

The graphic circle C logo is a registered trademark of David C Cook.

LCCN 2018940119
ISBN 978-0-8307-7641-2
eISBN 978-0-8307-7642-9

© 2018 Erika Pizzo
Illustrations © 2018 Josh Lewis

Designed by Josh Lewis
Edited by Laura Derico

Text set in Mrs Eaves and Boogaloo

Printed in Shenzhen, Guangdong,
China

1 2 3 4 5 6 7 8 9 10

050118

THE SAVING FARMER

WRITTEN BY Erika Pizzo ILLUSTRATED BY Josh Lewis

"And my God will supply every need of yours according to his riches in glory in Christ Jesus."

PHILIPPIANS 4:19 (ESV)

transforming lives together

There once was a farmer,
a very faithful farmer.
Every year that went by,
he worked harder and harder

He drove his tractor day after day,
planting and plowing till the sun went away.

The harvest was coming—
he just couldn't wait!
The sun was now setting,
and he was a bit late.

So the farmer started to turn back around,
when all of a sudden—what a terrible sound!

CLUNK
CLUNK
CLUNK

The tractor slowed to a stop.
"Oh, no!" cried the farmer,
"How will I harvest my crop?"

The farmer came home with a great, big sigh.
He thought about what happened,
and tried to figure out why.

"Daddy, what's the matter?" asked the farmer's son.
The farmer said, "I've plowed and I've plowed,
and now my tractor is done."

With a sad face and a heavy heart,
the farmer wondered where he should start.

The boy ran to his bedroom to find
a surprise that had just come to his mind.

**"Daddy, remember how I wanted this truck?
You told me to save, and that would be enough!"**

"I saved little by little
and bit by bit, every day.

My little grew to a lot,

and I bought it today!"

The farmer said, **"Son, you're right. I couldn't agree more! I'll start to save and see what God has in store!"**

The farmer began to save every day,
as his neighbors helped him harvest the hay.

After weeks upon weeks of waiting and waiting,

the farmer sat down to count up his savings.

1, 2, 3 ... 100, 101 ...

As the farmer continued to count it all up,
he realized the money just wasn't enough.

The farmer looked down, as he said with a frown,
"I am $1 short! What should I do now?"

Just then the farmer's son walked through the door.
He saw the look on his dad's face
and ran upstairs to a special hiding place.

He pulled out his favorite piggy bank
and reached in, all around.
Then he grabbed his four quarters
he'd been keeping safe and sound.

"I don't have much, but
what I have I'll give you.
After all, that's what
Jesus would do!"

The farmer hugged his son with tears in his eyes.
His kindness came as a wonderful surprise.

They both grabbed their coats and headed to the store,
where a brand-new tractor waited at the door!

With a little bit of saving
and God's help along the way,
the farmer bought his tractor —
and thanked God that day!

THE END